COVENANT KEEPER SERIES

Novel 1

PROPHECY
of the
RAVEN

Grant Hazen

PAGE PUBLISHING
Conneaut Lake, PA

First originally published by Page Publishing 2024

Fantasy Book Design by Moonchild Ljilja
https://fantasybookdesign.com/

ISBN 979-8-89315-922-6 (pbk)
ISBN 979-8-89315-936-3 (digital)

Printed in the United States of America

CHAPTER 1

A Pastor's Stand

I stood at the small lectern, the warmth of the early morning sun streaming through the windows of the Church of Solomon. The congregation had just begun to disperse after today's Sunday service, their murmured blessings and quiet footsteps fading into the hallowed silence of the church. As the last of the faithful filed out, I exchanged a few words with Mrs. Anderson, our longest-standing member, who always had kind things to say about the sermon.

"Thank you, Pastor Parable," she said, her eyes twinkling with warmth. "Your words always bring such peace."

I smiled, nodding. "I'm glad to hear that, Mrs. Anderson. Have a blessed week."

Taking a moment to absorb the peace of the now empty sanctuary, I made my way to the small study tucked away behind the altar. The scent of old parchment and candle wax filled the room with a calming embrace. My fingers brushed against the dusty spines of ancient texts, their secrets waiting to be unlocked.

The Church of Solomon, with its rich history dating back centuries, has always been a place of mystery and solace.

As if guided by some unseen force, my gaze fell upon a small wooden chest tucked away in the corner of the room. It seemed out of place amid the clutter, as if it were beckoning me to uncover its secrets. My curiosity piqued. I crossed the room and lifted the lid of the chest, revealing a single object nestled within—a golden ring, its surface etched with intricate symbols that shimmered in the dim light.

Hesitating for a moment, my hand hovered inches above the ring before succumbing to its pull and slipping it onto my finger. Instantly, a surge of energy coursed through me, awakening a flood of visions—an ancient temple, cryptic symbols, and the swirling forms of demons and spirits bound by shackles of immense light.

Before I could make sense of the torrent of images, a knock echoed throughout the church. I blinked, shaking my head to clear the haze. Carefully, I removed the ring and returned it to its small wooden chest, then made my way to answer the summons.

Standing on the steps of the church was a young woman, her eyes wide with fear and desperation. Rain soaked her clothes as she hugged herself in an attempt to keep warm.

"Please," she whispered, her voice barely above the sound of the rain. "I need sanctuary."

Without hesitation, I ushered her inside, wrapping her in a warm blanket I found in a nearby closet used for members of my congregation, and offered her a seat in the sanctuary.

"I'm Pastor Parable," I said softly.

"Rebecca," she replied, taking a seat on one of the many pews and clutching the blanket tightly around her.

"I'll make you some coffee. Please, Rebecca, do you mind telling me what ails you?" As I busied myself at the small coffee stand tucked between the two doors leading into the sanctuary from the vestibule, the bitter aroma filled the air. I listened as she began to speak, her voice trembling with fear.

She spoke of shadows that haunted her dreams and of voices that whispered unspeakable things she should do to those around her. Her words sent a chill down my spine, and I knew I could not turn her away, not when she had come seeking refuge in my family's church.

As I handed her a steaming cup of coffee, her eyes flickered with a strange light. The cup slipped from her grasp, shattering on the floor, and I watched in horror as Rebecca's demeanor shifted before my eyes. Her gentle features contorted into a grotesque mask of malevolence, her eyes gleaming with an otherworldly light. A rictus grin cracked through her pretty features.

A chill swept through me as I realized this young woman before me was no longer Rebecca but something far more sinister. Before I could react, she vanished in the blink of an eye, leaving me standing alone in the empty sanctuary. Then, as if from nowhere, her voice echoed through the sanctuary, seemingly from everywhere at once.

"Where is it, Jaydon?" she sang in a sing-song voice, her words dripping with malice. "Where is the Ring of Solomon?"

I stumbled backward, my mind reeling with fear and disbelief. How could this be happening? How could Rebecca, this innocent young woman who had come seeking sanctuary, be possessed by a demon? I may be a pastor, but I am nowhere near qualified to perform legitimate exorcisms.

As terror threatened to consume me, I felt the touch of the ring on my index finger. Its golden surface glistens in the dim light. A surge of ancient power welled up within me. With trembling hands, I reached out and touched it, feeling its warmth and power course through me.

"I—I don't know what you're talking about," I stammered, my voice barely above a whisper.

Rebecca laughed, a sound that sent shivers down my spine and echoed off the sanctuary walls. "Do not lie to me, Jaydon," she snarled, her voice echoing with a sinister resonance. "I can sense the ring's divine power within you. Give it to me, and perhaps I will spare your life."

I wanted to run, to flee from this unholy presence that now inhabited my sacred sanctuary. But before I could take a step, a blast of energy knocked me off my feet, sending me sprawling onto one of the wooden pews.

I struggled to regain my senses, the room spinning around me as I tried to make sense of what was happening. Then, as I looked up, I saw her walking down the wall from the ceiling as if she were merely taking a stroll through the park. In the next moment, she was standing before me, her eyes ablaze with a dark power I couldn't possibly understand.

"Take a seat, Jaydon," she commanded coldly. I tried to resist, to fight against the inevitable force that held me in place, but it was no use. With a sinking feeling in the pit of my stomach, I found myself being pushed down onto the pew, my body unable to move.

Rebecca approached, her form bathed in an otherworldly glow. "Now," she said, her voice dripping with venom, "where is King Solomon's Ring?"

I closed my eyes, a silent prayer on my lips as I grappled with the impossible choice before me. Should I give in to the demon's demands, sacrificing the power of the ring for the sake of my own life? Or should I stand firm, clinging to the hope that I could somehow overcome this unholy creature?

But even as the struggle raged within me, I knew there could be only one answer. With a steely resolve, I opened my eyes and met the demon's gaze, my voice steady despite the fear that gripped my heart like a vice.

"I will never give you the ring," I declared, my words ringing out with a sense of command and authority that surprised even myself. "It belongs to me, and I will not let you or anyone else take it from me."

The demon's eyes narrowed, and a flicker of anger crossed Rebecca's face. "Very well," she spat, her voice dripping with scorn. "If you will not give me the ring willingly, then I shall take it by force."

With that, she raised her hand, summoning a torrent of dark energy that surged toward me with terrifying speed. I braced myself for the impact, knowing that this would be the greatest test of my strength and courage yet. But just as the torrent was about to strike, I felt a surge of power emanating from the ring. I raised my hand and channeled the ancient power within me. As I did so, I heard a voice in my head cry out, and in defiance, I spoke the words aloud, "*Scutum fidei!*"

A barrier of brilliant light repelled the demon's attack, illuminating the gloom of the entire sanctuary before disappearing. For a moment, there was silence, broken only by the crackle of energy that surrounded us. Then, with a roar of inhuman rage, the demon launched herself at me, her claw-like nails bared and her eyes ablaze with fury.

But I was ready. With the power of the ring coursing through me, I stood my ground.

"By the power of the Lord, I command you, demon, be gone!" I cried, and with a final surge of strength, I unleashed the full force of the ring's power. The demon's spiritual essence was hurled out of Rebecca's body, consumed in a blaze of holy light.

As the darkness faded and the room regained its natural light, I found Rebecca lying on the floor, unconscious. Her face was serene in her slumber, finally freed from the demonic influence.

Catching my breath, my eyes were drawn to the nearby window, where a lone raven was perched, its eyes watching me with a keen intelligence that sent even more shivers down my spine. Before I could react, the raven spread its wings and took flight into the gloom of the rainy, early-afternoon sky.

CHAPTER 2

Secrets Unveiled

As the adrenaline from my conflict with the demon slowly ebbed away, I turned my attention to Rebecca, still unconscious on the floor. With a heavy sigh, I draped the blanket I had given her earlier over her to keep her warm until she awoke. My fingers absently rubbed the golden ring on my hand as my thoughts drifted to the ancient tomes and dusty manuscripts lining the shelves within my study.

The demon had claimed that this was the Ring of Solomon. According to legend, this ring was gifted to King Solomon by the Archangel Michael, bestowing upon King Solomon the ability to command demons and spirits, which he is said to have used to build his first temple in ancient Jerusalem. The idea that such a powerful and legendary religious artifact had somehow ended up in a small wooden chest in my family's church in the suburbs of Detroit, Michigan, seemed utterly implausible. Yet, I had just used it to banish a demon without even knowing how to wield its power. I had to know why.

Returning to the solitude of my study, I closed the wooden door with a soft thud behind me and breathed in the familiar therapeutic scent of old parchment and candle wax. I decided to start by examining the genealogical records I inherited along with the position of pastor after the passing of my late father. These records, meticulously kept by my familial predecessors, documented the lineages of scribes and holy men who had served this church, spanning centuries of my family's movements from one church to another. Somewhere within these fragile pages, I hoped to find a clue to the origins of my actual heritage.

Days, possibly even years, of research loomed before me in an attempt to learn whether or not King Solomon and I were related. Otherwise, I doubt I would have been able to access the ancient power of the ring with such ease. The research process threatened to drive me into a downward spiral into madness before I even began.

I sat at my desk, the golden ring now in my hand, looking it over curiously. The ring was covered in various intricate sigils. I recognized some of these sigils from my biblical studies as the names of both angels and archangels. Other sigils adorning the ring's golden body I did not recognize.

An inscription on the ring read, "The Seal of Solomon."

I slid the golden ring back onto the index finger of my right hand before continuing my search through my cluttered study. That is, until I came across an ancient pocket bible hidden away in a forgotten corner of one of the many bookcases surrounding my study. As I held the ancient pocket bible in my hands, a strange feeling told me the answer would be within its pages. But before I could open it, a knock echoed throughout the church once again. My heart beat faster as I stuffed the ancient pocket bible deep into the pocket of my dark gray peacoat and left the study to answer the summons once again.

At the door stood a man about my age, clad in a hooded jacket. His belt held various strange items attached by clips, though he made no move toward any of them. A long, thick, tattered fabric draped around his legs, revealing thigh-high work boots. On his shoulder perched a raven, the same one I had seen earlier watching from the window.

"Exhilarating! Absolutely exhilarating!" the mysterious man cried in excitement as he strode past me into the vestibule of the church, leaving me standing there blinking. "I have to say, you had me goin' there for a second, mate. I honestly thought I was going to have to intervene! But I wasn't expecting you to handle that demon as well as you did, and on your own, no less!" He continued, turning toward me as I closed the church door. "How did you do it, by the way?"

"I'm sorry, who are you?" I asked flatly, holding my hands up in a gesture of confusion.

"Ah! Right, right. Forgive me, Pastor. I'm Simon," he said, approaching me slightly bent over as if he were bowing, extending his hand for a handshake. "And this is my familiar, Corvin," he added, gesturing to the raven.

"Did you say familiar? As in a demonic spirit?" I asked, rubbing my fingers against the golden ring on my hand to ensure it was still there.

Simon closed his hand before suddenly standing up straight again. "Demonic?" Simon asked, glancing at Corvin, who returned his glance. "Ehh, can be, but no. Spirit? Well, technically, yes. My familiar is more of a faerie spirit than a demonic spirit. Similar type of entity, but from a completely different realm, I can assure you."

I immediately thought of Leviticus 19:31, which states, "Regard not them that have familiar spirits, nor seek after wizards, to be defiled by them."

"Simon, I think you should leave," I said calmly, re-opening the door for him.

"Alright," Simon said with a cheerful shrug, striding out of the church and back into the pouring rain. I sighed with relief as I closed the door behind him.

"Oh, I forgot. I was hoping you could help me out with something," Simon's voice said from behind me. Startled, I spun around to face him.

"How did you...? You know what? Never mind. But can I help you? No, no, no. I'm sorry, Simon, but as a pastor and a man of God, I am not supposed to associate myself with wizards," I said sternly, making my way toward the doors of the sanctuary.

Simon waited a beat before replying, "Do you think maybe if you consulted that ring of wisdom you've got there, you might reconsider your original consideration?"

I froze. "What do you know about the ring?" I asked guardedly.

"I know that it's not originally from this world," he said, strolling around the vestibule aimlessly. "I know that it's ancient and extremely powerful, and if placed in the wrong hands, it could unleash more chaos than either of us would want to deal with." He stopped walking and looked at me with a knowing smirk.

Simon certainly seemed to know far more about the Ring of Solomon than I did. "Alright, I suppose it wouldn't hurt to try," I said, raising my hand and focusing on the ring. I regarded the symbols and the six-pointed star on its golden surface. At first, nothing happened. I was about to tell him that when I started hearing barely audible whispering. Somehow, I understood what it was saying. My eyes grew wide as Simon watched, a knowing grin on his face.

"So, what's the verdict?" Simon asked, breaking my concentration. I blinked, returning my attention to him.

"What exactly do you need my help with?" I asked, still wary but intrigued.

"Excellent!" Simon said. "Why don't we sit down, yeah?"

I led Simon into the sanctuary, where Rebecca still lay on the floor beneath her blanket. As we passed her, I noticed Simon's face change with a brief hint of recognition as he glanced at her on our way past.

Simon and I sat together in the quiet of the sanctuary, the only sound coming from the rain striking the roof outside. The air was thick with the natural scent of old wood and used candles. As he began to explain, I listened intently.

"Pastor," Simon started, his playful demeanor turning serious. "I'll cut straight to it. There's a cult in Detroit. It started out small, so I didn't think much of it at first. But they've been growing in number."

I nodded, urging him to continue.

"I sent Corvin to follow a few of their members," Simon said. "Through Corvin, I overheard them mention a woman shrouded in darkness. They claim she is prophesied to rise with the blood moon and become their leader."

"They don't have a leader now? Who brought them together?" I asked.

"Witches. Members of the Coven of Detroit. All covens throughout the country are part of the Greater Coven. That's why I couldn't ask my brotherhood for help. They refuse to move against the Greater Coven because of a longstanding grudge. The Greater Coven still holds it against the Brotherhood of Wizards for not intervening during the witch burnings of the Inquisition."

A Brotherhood of Wizards and a Greater Coven of Witches have been feuding for years because of the witch burnings during the Inquisition. *Wonderful,* I thought sarcastically.

"You said this woman shrouded in darkness would rise with the blood moon? That sounds almost biblical," I said, stroking the stubble on my chin.

"I came to the same conclusion myself, which is why I sought someone with more knowledge on the subject. Unfortunately, I don't know any religious folk like yourself. Thankfully, I was informed of the demon in the area and planned to take care of it. Wouldn't you know it? It led me straight to you. Funny how that works, isn't it?"

"It is, yeah. God works in mysterious ways."

"So I've heard," Simon said with a respectful nod.

"Well, it just so happens that I might know someone who can tell us more about this woman shrouded in darkness and her connection to the blood moon," I said.

Simon's face lit up with playful excitement. "Then what are we waiting for? Let's go pay them a visit!" he said, jumping to his feet. Corvin returned to his shoulder from the wooden rafters above us. As I rose, I noticed Simon's expression suddenly shift to somber.

"Is something wrong?" I asked.

"Pastor, there's something else I need to tell you."

"Alright, let's hear it."

"I don't think you're going to like it, but you need to hear it. I had a vision. In it, you willingly succumbed to darkness. It consumed you. And I wasn't there to stop it."

His revelation struck me hard, and yet another chill ran down my spine. I remained silent, haunted by the implications.

At that moment, a soft moan broke through the tension. Rebecca, the young woman I had saved from demonic possession, was waking up. Her eyes fluttered open, confusion giving way to recognition as I approached her.

"Rebecca," I said gently, moving to her side. "It's okay. You're safe now."

"Pastor Parable?" she whispered. Her voice weak but clear.

"Yes," I replied with a reassuring smile. "Are you feeling alright?"

"I think so," she said as I helped her to her feet.

"My friend and I were just about to go out. Would you allow us to take you home?" I asked.

She nodded as Simon and I guided her out of the church. The heavy knowledge of the cult and Simon's troubling vision lingered in my thoughts, but I pushed them aside for now. Ensuring Rebecca's safe return home was our immediate priority. Then it was off to see an old friend who might know more about our predicament. The three of us climbed into my vehicle and pulled out of the church's parking lot onto the main road. Corvin followed close behind, his presence a silent reminder of the darkness we were up against.

CHAPTER 3

The Back Roads

As the car cut through the rainy gloom of the early afternoon, the music on the car radio turned into an unsettling static. Simon and I exchanged wary glances as the radio static intensified, filling the vehicle with a discordant cacophony even after I attempted to turn off the radio.

"What's happening?" Simon's voice cut through the eerie atmosphere, tense with apprehension.

"I'm not sure," I replied, my grip tightening on the steering wheel as the car's engine sputtered. With a jolt, the headlights flickered and the car lurched to a halt, leaving us stranded on a desolate backroad surrounded by looming trees.

Rebecca's eyes widened. "Why did we stop?" she asked weakly, her voice shaking.

"Stay here," I instructed Rebecca as Simon and I stepped out into the cold rain. Rebecca covered her ears as the radio static grew louder, punctuated by haunting voices in an unknown language.

"Do you hear that?" I asked, my heart racing.

"Yes," Simon confirmed, reaching for a thick, twisted twelve-inch stick clipped to his belt. "Something's not right."

In the fog ahead, a spectral figure materialized, its form shifting and flickering as if barely tethered to our reality. Dread washed over me as the entity's malevolent presence grew palpable. From the corner of my eye, I saw faint, shadowy figures flitting between the trees on either side of the road.

Rebecca peered out of the window, her face pale. "What is that?"

"Who are you?" I demanded, trying to keep my voice steady despite the fear gnawing at me.

The voice from the car radio crackled with malice. "Return the girl to us. She is one of four women shrouded in darkness. You cannot escape Coven's reach."

"We will protect her. Your power holds no sway here," I replied with defiance.

The witch's chilling laugh crackled through the static of the car radio as the wraith lunged forward, spectral tendrils extending from its form. Reacting swiftly, I raised my hand, the ring glowing faintly as I invoked its ancient power. "Stay back!" I commanded. The spectral tendrils froze and hung in the air like the tentacles of a squid before slithering back into the wraith.

I summoned the power of the Ring of Solomon once again, focusing my will. A surge of ancient energy and wisdom coursed through me, illuminating the ring with a brilliant light. With a wave of my hand, I commanded, "Be gone, wraith!" My words echoed with authority through the gloom. The wraith blocking our path vanished in a shimmer of light, forced to retreat by the power of my command. But before we could catch our breath, the shadow specters around us grew bolder. They moved with a purpose, closing in around us.

I watched in astonishment as Simon whispered something, and the twisted twelve-inch stick in his grip elongated into a twisted nine-foot staff, crackling with arcane energy. With a determined look, he tapped the twisted staff lightly on the pavement and cast a spell that sent a wave of arcane force rippling through the air, pushing back the encroaching shadows. The shadows hissed and writhed, their ethereal forms struggling against the combined might of our defenses.

"We need to move quickly," Simon urged, his voice strained with effort.

We hurried back to the car, the barrier of arcane energy holding the shadow specters at bay for now. With another whispered word, Simon's twisted staff retracted back into a twisted stick as he jumped back into the car and slammed the door closed. Rebecca was still in the back seat, safe yet clearly terrified and exhausted. She looked between us with wide, scared eyes.

"Pastor Parable? What's going on?" she asked groggily.

"Don't worry, Rebecca. You're almost home," I reassured her as I attempted to get the engine running, miraculously reviving it. I glanced at Simon, silently acknowledging the gravity of what we had just faced.

As we drove away, leaving the spectral encounter behind us, the barrier faded, its arcane energy spent. We drove in silence, the tension lingering in the air. I noticed Simon glance back at Rebecca through the rearview mirror.

"Do you think Rebecca could be the woman they mentioned? The woman shrouded in darkness?" I asked.

"It's possible," Simon conceded, "but the witches also said there were three more of them. Somewhere out there in the city."

The uncertainty gnawed at me as we neared Rebecca's apartment complex. We pulled into a parking spot in front of her building. Still too weak to do much on her own, we helped her out of the car, into the building, up the stairs, and down a hallway to her apartment door. I noticed her hands trembling as she fumbled with her keys. I gently took them from her and unlocked the door for her.

"Get some rest," I said softly as she stepped inside.

She nodded. "I will. Thank you, Pastor Parable," she said before closing the door and locking it.

"Before we go, I think we should leave a protection ward on her door," Simon suggested. "It'll ward off any evil trying to get inside."

I considered it for a moment, the ring on my right index finger whispering to me as I regarded its wisdom before nodding, "Do it."

Simon stepped up close to the door, placed his hand on its painted wooden surface, and began to whisper words of power as an intricate runic symbol began to materialize on the door. The lines of the symbol glowed faintly as he completed the warding spell, creating an almost palpable sense of protection over the entrance that I could actually feel even after the runic symbol disappeared into the apartment's threshold as he stepped back from the door.

"There, that should protect her and alert us if anything super-natural attempts to get inside," Simon explained, finishing his work.

Satisfied, we left the apartment building and returned to my car as the rain continued to fall. The weight of the afternoon's events pressed heavily on me.

"Jaydon," I said once we were inside the vehicle, holding out my hand toward Simon.

"What?" he asked, confused.

"My name is Jaydon. Jaydon Solomon Parable," I said, my hand still held out, waiting for him to shake it in an official greeting. Even though he was a wizard, I was starting to believe I could trust him. He did help fend off those specters on the back road our way here, after all. He even suggested we put up powerful protections around Rebecca's apartment so that nothing would harm her while we were away. Something I should have thought of myself.

Simon glanced down at my hand and smiled as he took it firmly. "It's nice to finally meet you, Jaydon Solomon Parable," he said.

With Rebecca safely returning home to her apartment, Simon and I continued on our journey through the rainy streets of Detroit. As we drove, Simon leaned forward slightly, his expression thoughtful.

"Hey, Jaydon," Simon began, his tone casual yet curious. "There's something I should mention."

I glanced at him as I drove, intrigued by the change in his demeanor.

"Sure. What is it?" I asked.

"When I saw you dealing with the whole demon situation back at the church, I realized that I think I know her."

My eyebrows furrowed in surprise. "Oh? Rebecca?" I inquired.

"Yeah," Simon confirmed, nodding. "Well, I'm pretty sure I know her brother."

I glanced at him, a mixture of surprise and curiosity coursing through me. "You know her brother? How?" I asked.

Simon leaned back in his seat, a thoughtful expression crossing his features. "Her brother's name is Daniel. He's a wizard, like me, except he's not involved with my brotherhood," he explained. "He was taken in by an auto-body repair shop run by other wizards in the area who taught him enchantment magic."

My curiosity piqued further. "An auto-body repair shop run by wizards?" I repeated, chuckling in surprise at the revelation.

Simon nodded. "They're well known in the supernatural community here in Detroit for their skills at enchanting cars to make them safer, among other things," he elaborated.

"If Daniel is her brother, does that make Rebecca a witch?" I asked.

"No. She doesn't have any magical capability. If she did, I would have known immediately," Simon said.

Although I appreciated his honesty, the knowledge that the supernatural world seemed to be much closer to home than I had ever imagined was unsettling. But the forefront of my mind still raced with questions about the mysterious cult, the impending blood moon, and why Rebecca was targeted by them.

With Simon's revelation weighing on my mind, we continued on through the rain-soaked streets of Detroit, our destination clear: to seek answers from my friend at the Detroit Cathedral. An old man named Father Emmanuel who may hold information about the impending blood moon and why it held such importance to the cult Simon mentioned.

CHAPTER 4

The Biblical Prophecy

The afternoon streets of Detroit were dark with gloom and drenched, the rain a relentless companion as we navigated the city's labyrinthine roads. The car's headlights carved paths through the gloom, illuminating glimpses of the urban landscape: dilapidated buildings standing as silent sentinels, their windows shattered like the eyes of the city's forgotten souls. Every now and then, we passed through pockets of light, where the city still breathed, alive with activity despite the hour.

We stopped at a red light, the glow reflecting off the wet pavement. I took a moment to study Simon. His profile was calm, but there was tension in his shoulders. A readiness that spoke of years spent navigating the supernatural underbelly of the city. I wondered what had brought him into this life and what stories lay hidden beneath his composed yet sometimes playfully mischievous exterior.

"You ever think about leaving all this behind?" I asked, breaking the silence.

Simon glanced at me, a faint smile tugging at the corner of his mouth. "Sometimes," he admitted. "But then I remember that there's always someone who needs help. Someone like Rebecca."

I nodded, understanding all too well the sense of duty that kept us tied to this shadowed world. The light turned green, and we continued on, the rain-slicked streets guiding us toward our next confrontation with the unknown.

We arrived at the Detroit Cathedral, its Gothic spires rising against the stormy sky like a fortress of faith amid the darkness. The old building was a stark contrast to the surrounding city, with its ancient stones holding secrets and stories that spanned centuries. We parked the car and stepped out; the rain was now a mere drizzle.

As we approached the massive wooden doors, I felt a sense of foreboding. Father Emmanuel was a friend, but he was also a keeper of biblical knowledge that was both righteous and powerful. If anyone could shed light on the blood moon and its connection to the cult, it was him.

Inside, the cathedral was dimly lit, the air thick with the scent of incense. Candles flickered in the alcoves, casting shadows that danced along the stone walls. We found Father Emmanuel near the altar, his back turned to us as he arranged the sacred items for the next day's service.

"Father Emmanuel," I called softly, not wanting to startle him.

He turned, his lined face breaking into a warm smile as he recognized me.

"Jaydon, my boy. It's good to see you." His eyes shifted to Simon, and he gave a slight nod.

"This is my friend, Simon," I said in introduction.

Simon stepped forward, offering his hand. "Father, it's an honor."

The old priest shook his hand firmly. "What brings you two here so suddenly?"

I explained what Simon had told me back at the Church of Solomon, as well as the events of this morning, detailing our encounter with the wraith and the ominous message from the witches. Father Emmanuel listened intently, his expression growing more serious with each word.

"The blood moon," he murmured, his eyes distant as he delved into his memories. "According to a biblical prophecy, the blood moon signifies the end times. In Joel 2:31, the prophet says, "'The sun shall be turned into darkness, and the moon into blood, before the great and terrible day of the *Lord* come.'" Father Emmanuel recited from memory.

My eyes grew wide as I realized what it meant. "The Antichrist," I said. Simon also appeared to be just as shocked to hear of this revelation as I was.

"But why Rebecca?" Simon asked. "What do they want with her?"

Father Emmanuel sighed, his gaze resting on the flickering candles. "Four women will play a pivotal role in the coming of the Antichrist. Rebecca is only one of them. They need a host for the Antichrist essence to imbue. This coven seeks to use her, as well as the three others, as pawns in their plans."

Simon's jaw tightened. "We can't let that happen."

"No, we cannot," Father Emmanuel agreed. "But you must be cautious. This coven seems powerful, and they will stop at nothing to achieve their goals. You must find these other women and protect them as well."

I felt the weight of Father Emmanuel's words weighing on my shoulders. This was bigger than I had imagined—a battle that stretched beyond our immediate comprehensions. But there was no turning back now. Rebecca's safety, as well as these unknown women's safety and possibly the fate of Detroit, not to mention the world itself, depended on our actions going forward.

"Thank you for your time, Father," I said, my voice resolute. "We won't let you down."

Father Emmanuel nodded as Simon and I left the cathedral. The rain had finally stopped, leaving the city washed clean.

"Jaydon?" Simon said, stopping just outside of the cathedral's doors, "How did Father Emmanuel know the cult needed a host for the Antichrist?" Simon asked.

I thought for a moment, "You know, I've learned that sometimes, some things are just better left unknown." I said, continuing on down the steps.

The path ahead was fraught with danger, but we were ready to face it. Together, Simon and I would confront the shadows that threatened our city and protect those who could not protect themselves.

CHAPTER 5

The Magic Touch

After I pulled my car into the garage, the scent of motor oil and rubber filled the air. The garage was a chaotic symphony of clanging metal, revving engines, and the hum of pneumatic tools. Fluorescent lights cast a harsh glow, highlighting the sheen of oil-streaked floors and the determined faces of mechanics engrossed in their work. Simon and I were greeted by a burly man named Jordan, his hands covered in grease, who asked how he could help us. Simon, sitting in the passenger seat, informed Jordan that we were there to see Daniel.

Jordan shouted across the busy garage to Daniel, a teenage boy with a smudge of oil on his face who was working on a car in the next garage over. He looked up and recognized Simon, giving him a nod before wiping his hands clean with a rag. He waved another mechanic over to continue working on the car, shouting over the many sounds that filled the garages, and joined us as we got out of the car to greet him. Simon introduced us to each other.

As the three of us stepped outside of the garage, away from the loud bustle, so that we could actually hear each other talk, Daniel's expression shifted from curiosity to concern as he listened to Simon mention his sister, Rebecca, and her predicament involving being possessed by a demon. The garage door closed behind us, muffling the sounds of industry and lending a momentary calm to our conversation.

Daniel's initial shock quickly changed to concern as Simon explained how I had banished the demon using the Ring of Solomon but that Rebecca was still in danger.

"Can I see it? The ring you used to save my sister?" Daniel asked.

I showed him the golden ring on my index finger. Proof that we were indeed telling him the truth.

"I can't believe it," Daniel muttered, his voice filled with worry. "Rebecca, possessed? Is she okay?"

"She's safe," I reassured him. "Simon and I dropped her off at her apartment after the whole ordeal. But she had previously come to my church seeking sanctuary. She was desperate, confused, and terrified."

"Well, that would make sense. She's never encountered anything supernatural before," Daniel said, his eyes darkening with concern as he processed what we were telling him.

"We believe her possession has something to do with a cult here within the city. A cult that has been growing in number lately. Have you heard anything about this?"

Daniel thought for a moment, his brows furrowing. "Now that you mention it, I do recall quite a few of my customers lately mentioning a cult known as the Cult of Lilith. Apparently, there have been whispers of strange gatherings and rituals taking place in some of the abandoned buildings turning up throughout the city. Some of my customers mentioned it in passing. Those who are part of the supernatural community anyway, but I didn't pay much attention to it at the time. Do you think these cultists summoned the demon that possessed my sister?"

"That's exactly what we believe," I said.

"Does Rebecca know about them? Does she know about the Cult of Lilith?" Daniel asked.

Simon shook his head. "Most likely not, no. We were careful not to tell her either. We're trying to keep her safe while figuring out the best way to handle this situation."

"We didn't want to scare her any more than she already was," I added.

Daniel let out a heavy sigh, his shoulders sagging with relief. "Thank you both for taking care of her. I can't imagine what she's going through."

"We'll do whatever it takes to keep her safe," I said sincerely.

Just then, I remembered the chilling encounter we had on the desolate back road while taking Rebecca home. "Daniel, there's something else I think you should know," I began, recounting the spectral encounter and the witch's voice speaking to us through the static of my car radio. "The witch's voice said that Rebecca was one of four women shrouded in darkness. It's as if we were being watched."

"She definitely seems to play a major role in this cult's plans," Simon added.

Daniel's eyes widened with concern. "I'll go see her after work. Maybe she knows something more than she's letting on. Maybe something could help."

A thought seemed to strike him as he continued, "You said it was like you were being watched? I might be able to help with that."

"Go on…" Simon said, prompting Daniel to continue.

"Well, if you think it would help, I could put an enchantment on your car that would prevent the cultists from keeping tabs on you. It might give you guys some breathing room while you continue to investigate them further."

Simon rubbed the back of his neck. "Well, it is Jaydon's car. And he isn't too fond of magic, if we're being honest," he admitted.

I considered the implications before making a decision. "I may not be fond of magic, but if it'll help us in any way, I'll allow it," I said reluctantly, unsure of whether or not this was truly the best decision.

Simon seemed surprised by my words as Daniel began going over payment for the enchantment.

As Daniel spoke, a troubling thought crossed my mind. "Daniel, have you noticed anything unusual here at the garage? Anything suspicious?"

Daniel hesitated for a moment before speaking. "Actually, there is this strange car that occasionally comes in here. The driver of the car keeps dropping off mysterious packages. I could feel a strange energy coming from within them. I thought it was a normal occurrence, but I can't shake the feeling that the whole thing seems shady."

Simon and I exchanged a glance. It seemed like we were uncovering more pieces of the puzzle with each passing moment.

"Keep an eye out for this strange car. The next time it comes into the garage, try to tag it with a tracking enchantment. Let us know if you do," Simon suggested.

Daniel nodded with a determined look in his eyes. "I will."

A new thought struck me: "Daniel, has Rebecca ever been here? Maybe recently?"

Daniel thought for a moment. "Yeah, she was here a couple of weeks ago. Why do you ask?"

Simon and I exchanged a knowing look. "It seems very likely that there might be someone working here who is helping the Cult of Lilith with their rituals," Simon said.

Daniel's eyes widened in understanding as the pieces began to fall into place.

"Thank you for the information, Daniel," I said, feeling a surge of hope. "Any lead, no matter how small, could be crucial."

"Be sure to keep a close eye on your coworkers. Let us know if you learn anything else that could help us," Simon added.

As we prepared to return to the car, Daniel's determination took hold. "I'll get that enchantment on your car now. It won't take long."

We followed Daniel to a workbench, where he had some tools and materials laid out. He began working on my car, drawing intricate symbols with a steady hand that seemed to glow silver, murmuring incantations under his breath. The process was fascinating, and though I was still wary of magic, I couldn't deny its usefulness.

While Daniel worked on my car, Simon and I discussed our next steps.

"Simon, we still need to find the other demonically possessed women," I said. "Maybe, just maybe, if we can banish the demon from within them too and keep them behind your protection wards, we might be able to prevent them from becoming the woman shrouded in darkness."

"Agreed," Simon replied. "Our priority is still Rebecca's safety, but we can't ignore the larger threat posed by this cult seeking the woman shrouded in darkness."

"But how are we even going to find them?" I asked, "These women could be anywhere within the city, and I highly doubt we'll just stumble upon them."

Simon nodded. "I know a place. A bookshop of sorts is here in the city. The owners are, let's just say, old-fashioned. I've frequented their shop plenty of times in the past. If there's anything we could use to help us find these other women, they're bound to have it.

"Good, let's start there," I said as we walked back over to Daniel. He had just finished applying the enchantment to my car and stepped back, wiping his hands on his jeans. "That should do it. Your car should now be shielded from any magical tracking."

I thanked Daniel, feeling a mix of gratitude and apprehension.

"We'll keep you updated on any developments regarding your sister," Simon promised as we jumped back into the car, started the engine, and pulled out of the garage as Daniel watched us leave.

CHAPTER 6

The Warlock's Wares

As Simon and I exited my car and made our way to the bookstore, he stopped me and said, "Listen, I'm sure you may already know this, but I thought I'd tell you anyway. This is no ordinary bookstore," he said.

My eyes narrowed as I looked over the small store wedged between two other storefronts. "It looks pretty ordinary to me."

"That's kind of the point," he said with a chuckle. "I just wanted to let you know so that you wouldn't be too surprised as to what you're about to see once we're inside."

"Who owns this place anyway?" I asked as Simon strode up to the door of the bookstore.

"You'll see," Simon said as he pushed the door open. A bell chimed as the air around us immediately thickened, buzzing with a subtle energy. Various books, artifacts, and other strange items loomed ominously from the shelves, casting elongated shadows in the dim light. Perched on Simon's shoulder, his raven familiar, Corvin, cawed softly, his beady eyes reflecting the store's eerie candle-lit glow.

The inside of the bookstore, if you could even call it that, looked nothing like it did through the storefront windows.

"Welcome, travelers," a voice said from the shadows deeper within the store. The disembodied voice startled me. The room seemed to ripple in response to the disembodied voice, with the shelves shifting as if moved by an unseen force. Corvin flapped his wings briefly, then settled back down, his gaze sharp and alert.

My pulse quickened, and my breath hitched at the display of magic. Unease gnawed at me; my faith had always taught me to view both magic and the occult with suspicion. Yet, here I was, completely surrounded by it.

Simon, unfazed, stood calmly amid the shifting shelves, his eyes calculating. He moved with an air of familiarity, as though he walked these paths daily. Corvin tilted his head, his intelligent eyes gleaming.

We navigated the shifting labyrinthine aisles, my gaze flitting from shelf to shelf, each brimming with strange books and even stranger artifacts. The shelves seemed to guide Simon as I followed his lead, rearranging themselves subtly to direct him. Corvin hopped from Simon's shoulder to a nearby moving shelf, pecking curiously at various items taken along with one of the moving shelves.

A glimmer of silver caught my eye as it sailed by one of the shelves. I reached out instinctively, my fingers closing around a small Star of David talisman. The moment I touched it, a strange sensation washed over me. A dormant power stirred within. The talisman resonated with the ring of Solomon on my index finger, causing the hair on my arms to stand on end. I held it up, marveling at its intricate design, adorned with similar symbols as those on the ring itself. The talisman gave off a faint glow.

"Simon, look at this," I called, my voice hushed. "It's a Star of David talisman. It feels like it's calling to me."

Simon turned, his eyes widening. "I doubt that's just an ordinary talisman," he said, his voice low.

"You would be correct," a disembodied female voice said from within the shadows of the bookshop.

"That seemingly ordinary trinket you've found there is the genuine article. Word has it that it once belonged to a descendant of King Solomon," a disembodied male voice said from the shadows.

My heart skipped a beat. Could this talisman be connected to my lineage? I thought to myself as I glanced between the talisman and the golden ring on my finger, lost in thought.

Simon disappeared within the shifting shelves. "Aha, here we go," I heard him say moments later. He strode back through the shifting shelves, holding a rolled-up scroll.

"What is that?" I asked.

"An interesting choice," said the female voice from within the shadows.

"That map is imbued with a small amount of dark energy. It will show you locations of more dark energy anywhere in the city. As well as in any other city, county, or suburb you happen to be in," the male voice said from within the same shadows.

"It's exactly what we need," Simon said, walking past me and up to a counter. A pair of figures emerged from the shadows behind the counter; these were the owners of the shop. The ones whose voices we've been hearing from the shadows. The man had a sharp, angular face and piercing blue eyes, while the woman had a more ethereal presence, her eyes a deep, mesmerizing green. If I didn't know any better, I would assume these people were warlocks, judging by their appearances.

Simon paid for the map and my talisman, exchanging cash and a strange blue feather with tips of turquoise. The warlock couple accepted the payment, their eyes glinting in the dim light.

"Thank you for doing business with us, travelers," the male warlock said, retreating back into the shadows.

"Please, come again," the female warlock said, also retreating into the shadows alongside her male counterpart.

Once outside the occult bookstore, I looked back and saw the bookstore for what it was—nothing more or less than an ordinary bookstore. I followed Simon to a nearby bench and took a seat. I took the Star of David talisman out of the pocket of my dark gray peacoat and hung it around my neck.

As I did so, I felt a subtle but powerful resonance with the ancient talisman. It was as if a current of ancient energy surged through me, imbuing me with a sense of warmth, protection, and purpose. Despite my initial skepticism toward the occult, I couldn't deny the palpable connection I felt to the talisman. Yet, I couldn't shake the lingering doubts that gnawed at the edges of my faith, leaving myself torn between two very different worlds.

As I adjusted the Star of David talisman around my neck, Simon took out the map and unrolled it before himself.

"Jaydon," Simon said, pointing to the map. "There are two locations marked with reddish-black energy. One of them is nearby."

Corvin hopped onto the back of the bench beside Simon, peering down at the map intently as I tore myself away from the Star of David talisman and peered at Simon's map. Its surface was indeed marked with representations of the city of Detroit. Dots of dark energy were scattered all throughout the city. I didn't realize how much darkness the city harbored among its busy streets.

I leaned in, my eyes narrowing at the tiny pulsating orbs spread around on the enchanted map. As my eyes located the nearest reddish-black orb nearby our current location, a strong sense of determination flared within me.

"Alright then, let's not waste any time," I said, my voice steady as Simon rolled up the map and tucked it away. His gaze fixed on the distant horizon where the sun began to set, painting the sky with a beautiful array of pink and orange hues amid a darkening blue sky.

CHAPTER 7

The Abandoned Warehouse

The enchanted map led us to the warehouse district. The crumbling facades and eerie silence of the area made my skin prickle with unease. Shadows danced under the dim streetlights, and the distant hum of the city felt far off.

As we approached the oldest and most decayed warehouse, a sense of foreboding washed over me. The air felt thick, almost tangible, with dark energy.

Without wasting any time, we entered the dimly lit warehouse. Immediately, Simon and I stood face-to-face with the possessed woman as she continuously scratched symbols into the walls and floor with bloodied nails. Her eyes, once filled with humanity, now glowed with otherworldly malevolence. Her hair hung over her face in a sickly, stringy display. With a guttural growl, she lunged toward us, her movements enhanced and twisted by the dark force that controlled her.

Simon, acting swiftly, drew an intricate symbol in the air before him as he spoke words of power, "Umbrae compedes." It must have been the wisdom of the Ring of Solomon, but somehow, I knew what he said. "Umbrae compedes," translated into English, was "shackles of shadows."

I watched as circular symbols shimmered into reality in the air before him in purple-black arcane energy, weaving shackles of the same purple-black arcane energy around the possessed woman's arms and legs, effectively restraining her from coming any closer.

"Jaydon, now!" Simon cried, sweat already beginning to bead on his forehead, struggling to hold her.

I clutched my hand bearing the Ring of Solomon into a fist, focusing on it as I closed my eyes. I attempted to speak the ancient prayers the ring whispered, but the demon fought against it. Its own voice echoed within my mind, attempting to drown out the words the ring attempted to whisper to me with its own cacophony of twisted words and mocking laughter. Yet, undeterred, I pressed on, deciding to try to use my own prayers instead. Still a beacon of light amid the suffocating darkness. With each word, bolstered by the ancient power of the ring, the demon writhed in agony. Its grip it on the woman's soul weakened as its essence began to unravel.

With a final "amen," my voice rose above the demonic cacophony within my mind, piercing through its attempts to prevent my exorcism. With a bone-chilling scream that echoed throughout the warehouse, the demon was cast out, banished from both the woman and the earth itself in a burst of black mist.

Simon gasped, releasing his spell. The circular symbols of purple arcane energy broke apart, unshackling the woman and allowing her to collapse onto her side on the cold floor of the warehouse.

I rushed over to her side, my heart pounding with relief and concern, to find her breaths shallow but steady. She stirred, slowly beginning to regain consciousness. The darkness lifted from her soul.

Simon squinted into the shadows of the warehouse. His intuition prickled; he closed his eyes and whispered a spell that cast an invisible ripple to flow throughout the inside of the warehouse from where he stood. The ripple of energy caused the thick, tattered fabric draped around his legs to flow outward briefly before fluttering back down around him. The spell alerted him to a sense of danger lurking hidden within the shadows.

"Jaydon…," Simon said in warning as two witches using gemstone wands cast aside the shadows they were using to conceal themselves in the corner of the warehouse. They strode forward, their faces twisted in grim determination as their gemstone wands gleamed off the outside lights that barely lit the warehouse.

One of the witch cultists made a *tsk tsk tsk* sound with her tongue as she came forward into the dim light.

"It seems our candidate didn't meet expectations as we would have liked," she said, casting a disdainful glance at the now-freed woman, disappointment flickering across her pretty features. "Such a waste of potential."

Her companion's eyes blazed with fury, her lips curling into a snarl. With a swift motion, she hurled multiple blasts of dark energy from different directions at Simon, her rage fueling her dark magic. But Simon, ever vigilant, deflected the attacks using his thick, twisted stick with multiple flicks of his wrist, sending the streaks of dark energy hurtling back toward their original caster. The witch screamed in anger as she swiped her gemstone wand, nullifying the spells before they could hit her.

The warehouse erupted into chaos as spells crackled through the air, illuminating the darkness with bursts of arcane and black magic energy.

"Scutum Fidei!" I cried, as the witch who had spoken of the freed woman with such disdain sent a streak of green electricity our way. My heart pounded in my chest as I held out my hand, casting a shield of holy light from the golden ring upon my finger. It deflected the green arcs of electricity hurtling toward the freed woman and me. The impact rang out, resembling the chimes of a church bell.

The freed woman watched the holy miracle before her eyes with awe, her eyes wide, stunned by what she was witnessing.

"Go!" I shouted to the woman, snapping her back to reality. My voice cut through the chaos with authority. With a terrified glance at the battle unfolding before her, she fled from the warehouse, seeking refuge in the relative safety of the night.

The witch, who had spoken earlier, exchanged a glance with her companion. Her lips curled into a cunning smile as she raised her gemstone wand high above her head.

"Enough," she hissed, her voice carrying an icy edge. The tip of her gemstone wand pulsed with a deep crimson light, casting an eerie glow that spread like a bloodstain through the dim space.

The second witch, still seething with rage, followed suit. Her wand shimmered with a kaleidoscope of colors before settling into a deep, pulsating blue. Together, they began to chant in a language older than the warehouse's decaying walls, their voices intertwining in a haunting melody.

Simon moved to intercept, but the witches' incantation reached a fever pitch. A swirling vortex of dark energy formed between them, the air around it distorting and vibrating with the raw power of their combined magic. With a final, triumphant shout, the witches directed the vortex toward the ceiling.

The roof of the warehouse split open with a deafening crack, sending debris raining down. Moonlight poured through the gaping hole in the ceiling, illuminating the witches in an ethereal glow. They exchanged one last glance, their expressions full of contempt.

The first witch smirked, her voice dripping with malice. "You think you've won something here? We have plenty of other candidates. This was merely a minor setback. An annoyance nonetheless."

In an instant, the witches were gone, their bodies dissolving into the swirling vortex that shot up into the night sky. The vortex collapsed behind them, leaving only a lingering echo of their chant and the faint, acrid smell of dark magic.

Simon lowered his thick, twisted stick to his belt, the warehouse now eerily silent in the aftermath of the battle.

"Jaydon?" Simon said quietly, searching the moonlit warehouse for me.

"I'm here," she said, stumbling out of the shadows and into the dim moonlight.

"Are you hurt?" Simon asked.

"Just some bad bruises," I replied, though my body ached from the impact of the falling debris. "You?"

"Bruised, but I'm alright," Simon said, wincing as he moved to inspect the extent of his injuries.

We both stood there, catching our breath. The tension of the battle slowly dissipated. The woman we had freed was long gone; hopefully the witches wouldn't pursue her further.

Simon examined our surroundings. "We need to get out of here before they decide to come back."

I nodded, but a pang of guilt struck me as I took in Simon's injuries. Blood trickled from a gash on his forehead, and his arm was already beginning to swell. I glanced down at my own battered body, the cuts and bruises throbbing with each heartbeat.

"Wait," I said, hesitating. "I want to try something."

Simon turned to me, curiosity mingling with skepticism. "What do you mean?"

I glanced at the ring on my index finger—the Ring of Solomon, an ancient relic passed down through generations, whispered about in hushed tones. I had never used it for healing before; its true potential was always a mystery.

"I've never tried this, but... we need to be in better shape if those witches decide to come back," I said.

Simon watched intently as I held up my hand, the ring's surface cool and smooth against my skin. I closed my eyes and took a deep breath, letting a silent prayer form in my mind, directing my thoughts and intentions toward healing.

A gentle warmth began to emanate from the Ring of Solomon, spreading through my hand and into my body. I opened my eyes to see a soft, golden light enveloping both Simon and me, bathing our wounds in its light. The pain began to ebb away, replaced by a soothing sensation that seemed to mend our injuries from within.

Simon stared at his now-healed arm, the swelling gone and the bruises fading. "Jaydon, how did you...?"

I shrugged, still somewhat in shock from the battle. "I... I just... I prayed."

For a moment, we stood in silence, the moonlight casting long shadows through the broken roof. The warehouse was a wreck, but we had survived.

Simon clapped a hand on my shoulder. "Well, it seems you've got a knack for this. It's almost like there's no limit to what you can do with that ring." He said, "Let's try to be more careful next time so that we're not injured even worse in the future."

"Agreed," I said, lowering my hand and feeling the ring cool once more. "But if we do, at least we know it works."

With that, we began to make our way out of the warehouse, stepping carefully over the debris.

The night was calm again, but the battle had taken its toll. As we walked back to the car, we decided to head back to the Church of Solomon and get some rest. We had a full day of searching for the other candidates the next day before the blood moon rose.

CHAPTER 8

Tailing the Night

The evening sky was painted in deep purples and blues as the mysterious car pulled out of the Magic Touch Garage, its black paint gleaming under the streetlights. Daniel, perched inside his own heavily enchanted car, watched with keen eyes. Simon had only asked him to put a tracking enchantment on the mysterious car, but Daniel had other plans.

The moment the mysterious vehicle rolled past, Daniel's car responded. He focused on two of the glowing runic symbols on his dashboard, causing them to flicker to life, confirming the enchantments were active. His car slipped into the street like a ghost, its presence masked by the enchantments he had painstakingly crafted.

Silence enveloped Daniel as his car glided along the asphalt. Not a single sound betrayed his pursuit. The car was not only enchanted to be silent but invisible as well, a trick he had mastered a year after he had first started working for the Magic Touch.

He trailed the mysterious car, maintaining a careful distance as they navigated the darkening streets of Detroit. The cityscape transformed as they drove deeper into its heart. The moonlight and artificial lights of the city reflected off of the looming skyscrapers above them as Daniel's mind raced with questions. Who was behind the strange deliveries to the Magic Touch? Using his knowledge of enchantment magic, he broke the protective spells on the packages in the Magic Touch's storage room to discover their contents. They were wrapped in old, enchanted seals, the kind that reeked of powerful, dark magic.

The mysterious car took a sharp turn, leading Daniel into a more desolate part of the city. The buildings grew older, and the air thickened with the scent of history and decay. Daniel's pulse quickened as the familiar facade of the Detroit Historical Museum came into view. The car he had trailed all the way here slowed and pulled into a side entrance, disappearing into the shadows behind the building.

Daniel was about to turn his car around and head home for the night, planning to contact both Simon and Jaydon the next morning, when he noticed someone standing outside the museum's front doors in the distance. The silhouette of a sharply dressed man with a mane of hair surrounding his head caught his eye.

As Daniel squinted through the front windshield of his car, it almost seemed as if this man was staring directly at him. But that was impossible. His car was still under the invisibility enchantment, and so was he while inside of it. For a second, he thought the enchantment had worn itself out, but the runic symbol on the dashboard still glowed and hummed with arcane energy. The only way someone could see through his invisibility enchantment was through the use of dark magic.

Daniel's heart began to race, a bead of sweat trickling down the side of his face. He shifted gears, deactivating both of the active enchantments with a thought as he sped away from the museum, his mind filled with a new sense of urgency as he raced home.

CHAPTER 9

The Enchanter's Revelation

I awoke the next morning in my room at the Church of Solomon, my body still aching from the events of the previous night, to find Simon awake in the sanctuary, already going over the enchanted map. Simon looked as tired as I felt, but we both knew there was no more time to rest. I made us coffee and moved to join him when his flip-phone rang. From his expression, I could tell it was urgent.

"It's Daniel," Simon said. "He wants us to meet him at the Magic Touch Garage. He says it's important."

We quickly gathered our gear and headed out. The drive to the garage was tense, both of us wondering what new twist awaited us.

When we arrived, Daniel was already there, pacing nervously outside.

"Hey, over here!" he called, waving us over.

"I managed to steal one of the packages without the cult's plant noticing. I figured out what they contained."

Inside the garage, Daniel led us to a table cluttered with various things you'd typically find at any old auto-body repair garage. A small, weathered box rested on the table among the clutter. He opened it to reveal several items—strange symbols etched into dark stones, twisted candles, and an amulet with a gemstone embedded in its surface.

"These are ritualistic items," Simon said, examining one of the stones.

"The cult must be using these to summon the demons we've been encountering," I added.

"That's not all I found out," Daniel said. "I followed that mysterious car using an invisibility enchantment. These packages are being sent by the director of the Detroit Historical Museum, Victor Blackwood."

Simon's eyes narrowed. "Vious," he muttered. "I suspected as much."

"Vious?" I asked, looking between Simon and Daniel.

"Victor Blackwood is also known as Vious in the supernatural underworld," Simon explained. "He's a powerful vampire, deeply involved in dark magic. Some say he has been collecting supernatural artifacts for centuries. If he's involved, he must be getting something from the cult in return."

Multiple thoughts rushed through my mind. The idea that vampires were real and that a powerful one resided here in Detroit, orchestrating these schemes alongside the Cult of Lilith, was terrifying.

"What do you suggest we do, Simon?"

"We need to stop these packages from reaching their destination," Simon said. "To do that, we need to confront Victor Blackwood himself."

"But if we're going after Blackwood, we can't just barge in unprepared," I said, looking at the artifacts Daniel had laid out. "If it's true that he has been at this for centuries, we'll need every advantage we can get."

"Which is why we're not going to just barge in. We're going to ask to meet with him."

Daniel stepped forward, his expression determined. "I'm coming with you," he said. "My enchantments could help."

Simon shook his head. "No, Daniel. It's far too dangerous. Blackwood isn't just a vampire; he's a master of dark magic. We can't risk you getting too caught up in this."

"Simon's right," I agreed. "We appreciate everything you've done, but we can't guarantee your safety."

Daniel's face fell, but he looked up with resolve. "Fine. If you won't let me come, at least let me give you a few things that might help. It could give you an upper hand if things go sideways."

Simon and I exchanged glances. "What do you have in mind?" Simon asked.

Daniel's face brightened. "Follow me."

We followed Daniel to a cluttered table typical of any old auto-body repair garage.

"First, these," he said, holding up a pair of black leather gloves. "They're imbued with a strong enchantment. You'll hit a lot harder, which might come in handy if things get physical."

I took the gloves and nodded appreciatively. "These will definitely be useful."

"And this," Daniel said, placing a hand on both Simon's and my shoulders. He closed his eyes and began murmuring words of power. We watched as his hands glowed silver. I realized he was enchanting my peacoat and Simon's hooded jacket. When the silver glow of Daniel's hands dimmed, Daniel looked up, satisfied with his work.

"I just enchanted your clothes with a durability enchantment," Daniel said.

"Thank you, Daniel," Simon said, as I nodded my thanks, unsure of how to feel about my peacoat having been enchanted.

Daniel smiled, though worry lingered in his eyes. "Just... look after yourselves, alright?"

"We will," Simon promised, clapping Daniel on the shoulder. "We wouldn't have gotten this far without you."

We said our goodbyes and returned to my car. Armed with a few new enchantments, we were prepared to confront Victor Blackwood, aka Vious. We drove off in the direction of the Detroit Historical Museum, the buildings and skyscrapers passing us by as we steeled ourselves for what lay ahead. As we drove, Simon glanced at me, his concern palpable. I knew I was tense, but I couldn't shake off the feeling of dread creeping over me. Before I could dwell on it too much, Simon's reassuring voice broke through my thoughts: "You alright?" Simon asked, "Don't worry, man. We've got this. We're in this together, remember?" His words eased some of my tension, reminding me that I wasn't alone in this fight.

CHAPTER 10

An Unexpected Encounter

As Simon and I drove toward the Detroit Historical Museum, the city's bustling streets seemed to blur past us. The afternoon sun cast long shadows, adding an eerie ambiance to our journey. We slowed to a stop at a red light behind a few other cars when, suddenly, our attention was drawn to a commotion up ahead. My heart began to race as I watched a disheveled old man bolt around the corner and tackle a well-dressed businessman carrying a briefcase to the ground.

"Another zombie? Ugh, stay here. I'll handle this," Simon sighed, as if he were annoyed by what was happening on the sidewalk ahead of us.

"Hold on, another what?" I asked, incredulous, as I ignored him, already following him out of the car.

The air outside was thick with tension. People cried out in a panic while running down the sidewalk to remove themselves from the terrifying scene. I could smell the city—exhaust fumes, street food, and something more pungent, a hint of decay that made my stomach turn. I watched as Simon reached for his belt, removing his thick, twisted stick from its clasp. With a swift motion and a whispered word, he elongated it into its staff form. The wood gleamed under the sun's light, and the runes carved into its surface glowed faintly as he approached the disheveled old man, who was attempting to take another bite out of the terrified businessman.

The disheveled old man's appearance was ghastly, his skin pallid and stretched taut over his bones. His eyes were clouded and devoid of life, and he moved with a jerky, unnatural gait.

Using his staff, Simon struck the creature in the head with a force that seemed almost supernatural, knocking it away from the businessman on the ground. I looked away as a few of the zombie's remaining teeth, as well as one of its eyeballs, fell out of its decaying head. The sound of the impact was sickening—a wet crunch that echoed down the street.

Simon then cast what seemed like a very simple spell, putting the tips of his fingers together at the point where his fingers met, held in front of the zombie's forehead. He then opened his hand while speaking a brief incantation that caused the zombie's body to convulse and then lay still. A dark-green mist rose from its body and dissipated into the air. Simon turned and walked back to the car with an air of calm, as if this were just another day at the office.

While Simon dealt with the zombie, I rushed over to the injured businessman who had been tackled. He was trembling, his eyes wide with fear, as he clutched at a gaping wound in his shoulder. The ring of Solomon on my index finger pulsed with ancient power. I could feel its warmth spreading through my hand, a comforting presence in the chaos. My heart pounded in my chest—a mix of adrenaline and fear. As I focused on the ring's energy, the chaos around me seemed to fade, replaced by a strange calm. Closing my eyes, I whispered a prayer of healing. Divine energy flowed from the ring, enveloping the injured businessman. His wounds glowed with a holy light as they closed, knitting together as if time itself were reversing.

As I healed the businessman, I watched Simon retract his staff back into a twisted stick with a whispered word as he walked back to my car. Meanwhile, the businessman's panicked cries began to subside, my healing prayer taking effect, restoring calm to the chaotic scene. He looked at me with a mixture of awe and gratitude, tears welling up in his eyes.

"How did you do that?" he asked, his voice trembling from the sudden near-death experience.

I gave him a reassuring smile and helped him to his feet, handing the shaken businessman his briefcase before returning to the car. Simon was already inside, waiting patiently.

"Zombies pop up every now and then," Simon explained as we continued on our way to the Detroit Historical Museum. "They try to spread their virus among the living. I honestly thought I had taken care of them all here in the city. It's been a long time since the last time I encountered one."

"Wait, you've done this before?" I asked, still processing the bizarre encounter.

"More times than I'd like to count," he muttered, resting the back of his head against the car seat. "It's just part of the job my brotherhood expects of me."

The rest of the drive was filled with an uneasy silence. My mind raced with questions. How many more of these creatures were out there? What other horrors lurked within the shadows of the city? And what kind of man exactly was Simon, that he could handle such monstrosities with such nonchalance?

As we continued our drive through the city toward our confrontation with the dark magic vampire, Victor Blackwood, I couldn't help but feel a sense of pride in our ability to confront danger head-on.

Although, to me, the city seemed much darker and far more dangerous now. I couldn't help but see every alleyway and shadowed corner of the city as a potential hiding place for the supernatural. Yet, despite the fear gnawing at the edges of my mind, with the ring of Solomon on my index finger, the Star of David talisman around my neck, and Simon by my side, there was also a thrill and a sense of purpose. Someone had to protect the people of this city from these creatures. The thought of Simon taking these monsters on alone for so long was surprising.

"Simon," I began, breaking the silence, "how did you get into this line of work?"

He glanced at me, his eyes serious at first, as if recalling a bad memory from his past, before softening.

"It's a long story, Jaydon. Maybe one day I'll tell you. But for now, we have something far more important to focus on."

I nodded, understanding that some stories were best saved for another time. As the Detroit Historical Museum loomed into view, I steeled myself for whatever lay ahead. The world was darker and more terrifying than I had ever imagined, and I was right in the middle of it, ready to face whatever came next.

CHAPTER 11

Confronting Blackwood

The Detroit Historical Museum loomed ahead, a bastion of history standing firm amid the chaos of the city. Its stone facade, weathered by time, contrasted sharply with the surrounding modern buildings.

Inside, Simon and I approached the customer service desk, our nerves masked beneath what I hoped came across as a casual inquiry.

"Good afternoon," Simon said, his voice smooth. "We'd like to speak with Director Blackwood."

The receptionist, a middle-aged woman with kind eyes, looked up from her computer. "Do you have an appointment?"

"No," Simon admitted, "but it's rather important. We were hoping he could spare a few minutes."

The receptionist hesitated, glancing at the phone on her desk. "Mr. Blackwood is currently in a meeting, but I'll see if he can fit you in."

As she made the call, I looked around the lobby. The museum's hushed atmosphere, with the soft, echoing footsteps of visitors and the distant hum of air conditioning, did little to ease my anxiety. It felt as if the very walls were watching us, aware of the confrontation to come.

"Mr. Blackwood has agreed to see you once he finishes his current meeting," the receptionist said, hanging up the phone. "Please, have a seat. It shouldn't be too long."

"Thank you," I said, my voice barely masking the tension I felt.

We settled into the museum's plush lobby chairs, the weight of our mission pressing down on us.

"This is it," Simon murmured under his breath.

I nodded, my heart pounding in my chest. "We need to be ready. I have a feeling he's not going to make this easy."

As we waited, I removed the ring of Solomon from my finger, the feeling of its ancient energy coursing through me lifted, and placed it carefully into the pocket of my black dress pants before reaching into the pocket of my peacoat. I pulled out the enchanted gloves Daniel had given us back at the Magic Touch Garage. The leather was soft, almost warm to the touch, and as I slipped them on, I felt a subtle surge of power course through my fingers.

Simon watched me with a knowing look in his eyes.

"Better to be prepared," he said quietly.

I nodded in reply, flexing my fingers. The gloves felt like an extension of my hands; Daniel's enchantment woven within them enhanced my strength and sharpened my senses.

Minutes stretched into what felt like hours. The ticking of a nearby clock was a constant reminder of the impending confrontation. Finally, the receptionist motioned for us to follow her.

We followed her through the museum, past exhibits that chronicled the city of Detroit's storied past. The weight of history is pressing down on us. As we walked, my eyes wandered over the exhibits. To our right, a diorama depicted Detroit's bustling automotive industry in the 1920s, complete with miniature assembly lines and tiny figures laboring over early model cars. The scene was vibrant, capturing the spirit of innovation that had once defined the city.

Further along, we passed a poignant display dedicated to the Underground Railroad. Mannequins in period attire stood frozen in a moment of desperate escape, their eyes wide with hope and fear. The background was painted with a dense forest, symbolizing the treacherous journey to freedom. Plaques beneath the figures detailed stories of bravery and survival, reminding visitors of the city's critical role in the fight against slavery.

In another exhibit, gleaming cases housed artifacts from the Prohibition era. Flapper dresses, vintage cocktail shakers, and sepia-toned photographs of clandestine speakeasies gave a glimpse into a time of roaring defiance and hidden revelry. One photo caught my eye—a grainy image of a police raid, the tension in the scene eerily mirroring our own covert mission.

As we turned a corner, a massive mural dominated the wall. It depicted the 1967 Detroit riot, a chaotic blend of flames, protestors, and police, capturing the city's tumultuous struggle for civil rights. The raw emotion in the mural's faces, the fury and despair, felt almost tangible, resonating deeply with the current unease I felt.

We entered through a door that read, staff only, and down to the end of a long hallway. Finally, we reached Blackwood's office. The door, a heavy oak structure, seemed to swallow the light, adding to the ominous feeling in the pit of my stomach.

The receptionist knocked lightly, then opened the door, ushering us in. "Mr. Blackwood, these are the two gentlemen who have come to see you."

Victor Blackwood himself rose from behind his imposing mahogany desk, his presence filling the room. He wore a black suit with a striking red tie, the vivid color slashing through the blackness of his suit like a blade. His mane of jet-black hair framed a face that was both handsome and intimidating. But it was his eyes that held me captive—icy blue and piercing, they seemed to see right through me.

"Welcome, gentlemen," Blackwood said, his voice deep and smooth. "Please, have a seat."

Simon and I sat down, the leather chairs creaking slightly underneath our weight. I could feel Blackwood's eyes on us, scrutinizing and assessing as he returned to his seat behind his desk.

"What brings you gentlemen to my museum without an appointment?" he asked, a hint of curiosity in his tone.

Simon leaned forward, carefully choosing his words. "We've been looking into some recent… unusual events around the city, and your name happened to come up. We were hoping you could help us understand a few things."

Blackwood's expression remained neutral, but I noticed a flicker of something darker in his eyes.

"Unusual events? I'm afraid I don't know what you're referring to."

"Artifacts," I interjected, keeping my voice steady. "Certain items have gone missing from your museum."

For a moment, the room was silent, the air thick with tension. Blackwood's facade of polite interest slipped momentarily, replaced by a hardened glare.

"I see," he said slowly, his voice dropping the hint of a menacing tone. "And you think I have something to do with this?"

Simon and I exchanged another glance, silently preparing ourselves for what was to come. This was no ordinary conversation, and Blackwood was certainly no ordinary man.

"We're just following the evidence," Simon replied, his tone measured. "If you could answer just a few of our questions, it might help clear things up."

Blackwood leaned back in his chair, his eyes narrowing. "Very well. Ask your questions. But I warn you, I do not appreciate baseless accusations."

Carefully navigating the conversation, we probed Blackwood for answers without revealing our hand. Simon kept Blackwood engaged with pointed questions while we observed his reactions closely, looking for any slip that might reveal the truth.

"Mr. Blackwood, these artifacts have a significant impact on the city's history and safety," Simon said. "Surely you understand the importance of ensuring they don't fall into the wrong hands?"

Blackwood's expression hardened, his icy blue eyes turning colder. "I assure you, everything in this museum is well-protected."

"And yet, several pieces have still gone missing," I said, leaning forward. "Pieces that hold immense power." As black wood rose from his desk, his movements slow and deliberate, Simon and I instinctively stood as well, our bodies tense with anticipation.

Blackwood's calm demeanor turned to rage in an instant. He moved with a supernatural speed, seizing me by the throat with a grip of iron. The next thing I knew, he had me slammed up against the wall of his office with a force that threatened to break bones.

Thankfully, my enchanted peacoat absorbed much of the impact, sparing me from more serious injury.

"Enough!" he snarled, his eyes burning with malevolent power.

"Let... him... go," Simon ordered, pulling his thick, twisted stick from his belt and leveling it at Blackwood.

Drawing strength from the enchanted gloves, Blackwood watched, confused, as I pried his supernatural vice-like grip free from around my throat.

As I pulled his iron grip away from around my throat with ease, the Star of David talisman I wore around my neck began to glow. The light grew in intensity before releasing a shockwave that sent Blackwood sprawling across the room. He crashed into a display case, the impact shattering the glass and sending the contents of the display case scattering across the floor.

"How did you do that?" Simon asked in amazement, lowering his twisted stick.

"I—I have no idea. It just—just happened on its own," I said, rubbing my throat and taking in deep gulps of air.

Blackwood stirred from within the remnants of the destroyed display case. His energy seemed to be spent. He slowly returned to his feet as Simon leveled his twisted stick at him once more, prepared to cast if necessary.

"Answer our questions, and this ends peacefully," Simon commanded, his voice steady, but I could sense the underlying threat.

Blackwood glared at us, brushing bits of glass and debris from his well-tailored suit.

"We know about the shipments to the Magic Touch Garage," I said, my voice still hoarse from the earlier chokehold. "How many more are planned to go out?"

Blackwood's face twisted into a grin, equal parts madness, satisfaction, and triumph.

"The last one has already been sent."

"Why there?" Simon asked, eyes narrowing, "Why use the garage?"

"The garage is nothing more than a front," Blackwood admitted, his voice dripping with disdain. "The Cult of Lilith has been using it to move the artifacts without drawing any attention.

I stepped forward and said, "Why are you helping them? What's in it for you?"

"More Power. More Influence. They promised me a place of authority in the new world they plan to create," Blackwood admitted.

"And you think they'll spare you now?" I asked, "Now that their supplier has been caught?"

"Like I said, the final shipment has already been sent. I've already done my part," Blackwood said, returning to the chair behind his mahogany desk.

My stomach tied itself into a knot, hoping we weren't too late to intercept the final package.

"What do they plan to do with the final shipment of ritualistic artifacts?" I asked.

"The final shipment contains the last pieces they need for their final ritual," Blackwood explained. "They're planning to summon a being of immense power. A being that will bring peace and prosperity to their new world order."

The weight of Blackwood's words hit Simon and me like a truck as we glanced at each other.

With a heavy heart and a sense of defeat weighing me down, we left Blackwood's office, knowing deep down that we had failed to stop the Cult of Lilith's plans. The truth of Blackwood's revelation lingered in my mind like a bitter taste, a stark reminder of the imminent danger looming over our city. Simon and I returned to my car and made our way back to the Magic Touch Garage to inform Daniel of our failure.

CHAPTER 12

Shadows over Berkeley

My heart sank alongside Simon's as we realized we'd failed to intercept the package. It was now in the hands of the Cult of Lilith, with their plans moving forward at an alarming pace. The weight of our failure pressed down on us as we drove back to the Magic Touch Garage, the air thick with urgency. The enchanted leather gloves I had worn back at the museum are now replaced by the Ring of Solomon on my right-hand index finger.

Daniel looked up from his work, his eyes widening at our expressions as we entered the garage.

"What's wrong? Did you get the package?"

I shook my head, frustration evident in my voice. "We were too late. The cult has it now."

Daniel's face grew grim. "What's next, then?"

Simon clenched his fists. "We need to track down their next candidate. If we can stop them from finding a host for the woman shrouded in darkness, we might still have a chance to stop their final ritual."

I nodded my agreement as Simon drew the enchanted map from his belt. Unfolding it carefully, he laid it out on a nearby workbench. The ancient parchment glowed faintly, illuminating points of dark energy located throughout the city of Detroit.

Simon pointed to a spot on the map. "Here," he said, his voice tense, "the map shows the cult's next candidate is in Berkley, a northern suburb of Detroit. We need to get there, and fast."

Daniel's face tightened with worry, but he nodded.

"Just… Promise me nothing will happen to my sister," he said.

"We'll continue to make sure she's safe," I assured him, though the weight of the promise hung heavy on my shoulders. We had already failed once today.

Leaving the Magic Touch Garage, we climbed back into my car and sped off, the city's grim skyline soon giving way to the quiet suburbs of Berkley.

House after house, we drove past manicured lawns and neat driveways, the serene neighborhood a stark contrast to the chaos we were trying to prevent.

The map led us to a specific house, an ordinary-looking place. It was the type of home someone would start a family in. The normalcy of it was almost surreal, given what we knew. It definitely didn't scream—the demon's lair, that's for sure. I parked the car a little way down the street, and we both took a moment to steel ourselves.

"This is it," Simon said, more to himself than to me.

We approached the house cautiously, the late afternoon sun casting long shadows across the lawn. My heart pounded as we reached the front door, each step echoing the urgency of our mission. Simon reached out and knocked, the sound seeming unnaturally loud in the quiet neighborhood. He attempted the doorbell, but still nothing. No one answered, but the sense of dread was palpable. It was the kind of silence that felt wrong, as if the house itself was holding its breath. Simon and I exchanged a glance. He placed his hand over the doorknob, muttering an incantation under his breath. The lock clicked open with an eerie finality, and we let ourselves in.

The sight that greeted us made my stomach churn. The living room was a wreck—broken furniture, shattered glass, and what looked like claw marks on the walls. It was clear that something violent had taken place. The air was thick with the metallic tang of blood, mingling with the stale scent of fear.

"Stay close," Simon whispered, though it seemed unnecessary. I had no intention of wandering off.

We moved through the house cautiously, the floor creaking beneath our feet. The kitchen was in a similar state of disarray—cabinets flung open, their contents strewn across the floor. My eyes were drawn to the bloodied claw marks on the walls, a chilling testament to the struggle that had occurred.

A noise from upstairs caught our attention. It was a low, guttural sound, halfway between a growl and a sob. We exchanged a tense glance before making our way up the staircase.

As we reached the top of the stairs, the sound grew louder and more desperate. The hallway was dimly lit, and the walls were covered in those same strange symbols that glowed faintly with a sinister light. The same ones Daniel had said Rebecca had dreamed of.

My heart pounded in my chest as we approached the source of the sound. The sight before us was nothing short of horrifying. The woman was hunched over, her fingers clawing at the door in front of her, carving those same symbols into it. Her hands were raw and bloodied, and her fingernails were torn. The hallway was already covered in the symbols, a testament to her relentless, mindless effort.

Suddenly, I heard a faint sob coming from inside the door.

"Simon," I whispered, "I think there's a child in that room." Simon's eyes hardened with determination as he took in the scene. The woman, clearly possessed, turned her head at an unnatural angle to look at us, her eyes glowing with malevolent energy. She let out a guttural snarl, her body convulsing as she rose to her feet.

"We need to act fast," Simon said, his voice low and urgent. He raised his thick, twisted stick, arcane energy crackling at its gnarled tip.

The possessed woman hissed and lunged at us with inhuman speed. Simon swung his stick, releasing a burst of arcane magic—a shimmering wave of force intended to subdue her. But she moved with an unnatural agility, dodging Simon's spell. In a sickening display of demonic prowess, she crawled up the walls and onto the ceiling, her limbs bending at impossible angles.

"Jaydon, get ready!" Simon shouted as he unleashed another spell from his stick, arcs of lightning dancing from its tip. This time, the bolts struck the ceiling, forcing the woman to drop to the floor. But she was quick, rolling to her feet and baring her teeth in a feral grin.

I stepped forward, the Ring of Solomon glowing on my index finger. The whispers seemed to fill the air, a soothing counterpoint to the woman's growls and snarls.

The possessed woman let out a scream that echoed throughout the house—a haunting, guttural wail. She lunged at me, eyes blazing with malevolent fury. Simon's reflexes were sharp—his stick flicked upward, conjuring a shimmering barrier of arcane energy. The woman collided with it mid-air, her body contorting and writhing in a desperate attempt to shatter the barrier.

"Keep it up, Jaydon!" Simon urged, his voice strained as he struggled to maintain the barrier. My whispers grew louder and more insistent. The symbols on the walls began to glow brighter, and the air thickened with the tension of the spiritual battle.

With a final, desperate scream, the woman broke through the barrier, shattering it like glass, and charged at me. Simon reacted instinctively, raising his stick and unleashing a torrent of energy that wrapped around her like chains. The arcane bonds tightened, but the possessed woman's fury made her stronger. She strained against the bonds, inching closer to me.

My prayers reached a fever pitch, the Ring of Solomon blazing with light. I extended my hand, a pulse of energy erupting from the ring, striking the possessed woman. She convulsed violently, her screams mingling with the demonic roars that filled the room.

In a blinding flash, a burst of black mist erupted from the woman's body. The mist coalesced into a hideous, shadowy form before dissipating into nothingness. The woman collapsed to the floor, unconscious but free from the demon's influence.

The house was quiet, except for the soft crying coming from inside the locked room. The oppressive atmosphere lifted. Simon and I exchanged a weary glance, both of us exhausted but relieved. We had succeeded, at least for now.

Simon waved his twisted stick before returning it to its clip at his belt, the spell unlocking the door where the sounds of crying were coming from, before he knelt beside the woman. He checked her pulse. "She's alive," he said, his voice tinged with relief.

I nodded, glancing at the door the woman had been clawing at. I carefully opened it, revealing a young child huddled in the corner of a bathtub. His face was streaked with tears, and his eyes were wide with fear.

"It's okay," I said softly, stepping into the room. "You're safe now."

The child hesitated but then ran to me, clinging tightly to my peacoat. I held the child close, his small body trembling against mine. The feeling of his tears soaking into my peacoat grounded me amid the chaos we'd just endured.

I glanced back at Simon, who was helping the woman into a sitting position, her eyes slowly fluttering open.

"It's over," I whispered, both to the child and myself. "You're safe," I repeated.

The woman stirred, her gaze slowly focusing on Simon, then on me. "Who—who are you?" she asked, her voice weak and shaky, "What are you doing in my home?"

Simon gently helped her to her feet, steadying her as she wobbled.

"My name is Simon, and this is Jaydon," he explained softly. "We were passing by when we heard a commotion. There was a robbery," Simon lied, "and it looks like you were hit hard on the head while trying to get your child to safety."

Her eyes widened as she took in the wreckage around her, her hands rising to her temples as she tried to piece together the fragmented memories.

"A robbery? I—I don't remember…"

"You were incredibly brave," Simon lied, his voice soothing. "But it's over now. You're safe."

She looked at him, confusion and gratitude mingling in her expression.

"My son… is he…?"

"He's okay," I reassured her, feeling the child's grip tightens. "You're both safe now."

Tears filled her eyes, and she managed a shaky smile. "Thank you. I don't understand, but thank you."

Simon nodded, his expression solemn. "I recommend you call the authorities."

She nodded weakly, her eyes filled with a mix of relief and exhaustion. "I will, thank you," she repeated, her voice barely above a whisper.

As Simon spoke to the woman, I noticed that the symbols on the walls had vanished along with the demonic spirit.

Simon and I stepped out of the house, closing the door behind us.

Simon placed a protection ward on the door before we hurried back to the car, the sun now dipping below the horizon. The sky was painted in shades of red and gold, the impending blood moon casting an eerie glow. We had little time to reflect on our victory; the urgency of our mission pressed heavily upon us.

As we got in, Simon unfolded the map again.

"There's still one more candidate," he said, tracing his finger over the glowing spots on the enchanted map. "We have to hurry."

I nodded, starting the engine and pulling away from the curb. The drive was tense, and the weight of our task was pressing heavily on us. The city blurred past, and the looming presence of the blood moon was a constant reminder of the limited time we had left.

We navigated through the streets once again, finally arriving at our final destination.

CHAPTER 13

The Forsaken Tunnels

"Are you sure this is the right place?" I asked as we got out of the car.

"It's where the map led us to," Simon replied, closing the passenger side door with a decisive thud.

We stood before an abandoned concrete bridge, its surface covered in graffiti and overgrown with vines from the surrounding trees.

Once, cars drove both over and under this bridge, but new roads had left it abandoned and forgotten. The air was damp and filled with the earthy scent of decaying leaves, adding to the sense of desolation.

Simon closed his eyes and spoke a word of power. A ripple of energy flowed through the immediate area, sending the thick, tattered fabric around his legs to flow outward momentarily before draping back around them. When he opened his eyes, he pointed to a hidden passageway underneath the bridge, concealed in shadow.

"She's definitely here. There's a hidden passage way underneath the bridge," Simon said, his voice tinged with unease.

"Hold on a second, Simon," I said, reaching for his shoulder as he started forward. "Let me pray for us first."

"Good idea." Simon bowed his head and clasped his hands together.

I took a deep breath, centering myself as I reached into my pocket and pulled out the ancient family pocket bible. I flipped through its delicate pages until I found the prayer I was looking for.

"Heavenly Father, as we stand on the brink of the unknown, entering the valley of the shadow of death, we call upon Your divine protection. Though darkness surrounds us and danger lurks in every shadow, we trust in Your unwavering presence."

As I prayed, a warm, comforting energy flowed through me. The ring of Solomon on my finger and the Star of David talisman around my neck began to resonate with each other, both glowing softly and casting a faint light that enveloped both myself and Simon. The light formed a thin, shimmering barrier around us, a sense of security and hope rising within us.

Simon watched as the protective glow surrounded him, his grip on his twisted stick relaxing slightly. I looked up from the pocket bible, feeling a strong sense of protection I had not felt earlier.

"We're ready," I said firmly, returning the pocket bible to my pocket. He nodded, his expression a mix of determination and gratitude.

"The demon is inside those tunnels," Simon said, more sure of himself than before. "Stay on your guard."

I nodded as we made our way to the hidden passage underneath the bridge.

The tunnel led to a winding concrete staircase descending into another, darker yet shorter tunnel that seemed to end in a pitch-black concrete room, out of reach from the light of the setting sun outside. The air grew colder as we descended, and I could hear the distant drip of water echoing through the passageway.

Simon removed his thick, twisted stick from his belt and whispered a word of power, "Choris luminum."

Choris luminum in Latin is translated to dance of lights.

Four orbs of radiant energy began to materialize in the air before us, each pulsating with a soft, ethereal glow. As Simon focused on the spell, the orbs solidified, hovering in place and casting flickering shadows across the walls of the concrete hallway.

With practiced precision, Simon directed the lights to dance and weave through the air in a mesmerizing display. It was as if he were conducting an invisible orchestra. The lights swirled and twirled like spectral dancers, casting patterns of both light and shadow that illuminated every corner of the large concrete room ahead.

In the lantern-like light of Simon's spell, we saw the walls of the large concrete room covered in more of those strange symbols. The same ones we had seen before haunted us from our previous encounters with the other candidates.

This time, the symbols were far more cryptic, twisting in unnatural patterns that seemed to pulse with malevolent energy as if they were alive.

Simon took a deep breath, the lights reflecting in his eyes as we stepped forward, the orbs illuminating our path, casting eerie shadows that seemed to move on their own.

As we entered the large room, the air grew even colder, and a low, guttural growl echoed from the shadows. In the center of the room lay another woman, her body convulsing and her eyes glowing with an unnatural red light. The demon within her was fighting for control.

Simon spoke another word of power, his voice steady and commanding. "Exsilium," he intoned. The orbs of light intensified, focusing their beams on the woman, their radiant energy pushing against the demonic force within her.

The woman screamed, a sound that was both human and otherworldly. Her body lifted from the ground, hovering as the battle between light and darkness raged within her. I could see the strain on Simon's face and the effort it took to maintain the spell. He wouldn't be able to hold it for long.

I joined in, raising my hands and calling upon the power of the ring. "In nomine Dei, exorcizamus te," I chanted. I knew nothing about performing exorcisms, but it was as if the ring of Solomon were guiding me and telling me what to say. I could feel the ancient power flow through me. The room shook, and the symbols on the walls seemed to writhe in agony.

The demon fought back; dark bolts shot from the woman's body, attempting to extinguish the orbs of light. Simon continued to conduct them, causing the orbs to dance and weave out of the way of the bolts of dark energy. His voice grew louder and more insistent. We both put everything we had into saving this woman and banishing the demon from within her.

With a final, ear-splitting scream, the woman fell to the ground. A dark mist exploded from her body as she hit the concrete floor, dissipating into the ground around her. Her eyes were wide, yet lifeless and still. The room was silent, save for our heavy breathing.

Simon knelt beside her, checking for a pulse, but there was none. Simon closed his eyes.

"Her soul..." he whispered. His voice filled with sorrow. "Jaydon, she's gone."

I looked around the room; the symbols had now faded and were powerless. "But... but we banished the demon," I said. "It's gone, isn't it?"

Simon stood; his expression grim. "The demon is gone. We banished it, but it took her soul along with it." He paused for a moment before adding, "We can't leave her like this."

Suddenly, the ring of Solomon began to whisper to me. The Star of David talisman around my neck vibrated violently.

My eyes grew wide, understanding what the ring was telling me.

"What is it? Jaydon, what's wrong?" Simon asked, concern evident in his voice.

"Stay with her! I'll find you!" I cried, bolting from the room.

"Jaydon, wait!" he called after me as I dashed up the winding concrete staircase. Throwing myself outside of the concrete tunnels, I raced out onto the abandoned road.

It was dark, but the blood moon was impossible to miss. It loomed overhead, large and foreboding, in the night sky. We were too late.

CHAPTER 14

The Woman Shrouded in Darkness

As I stood in the middle of the abandoned street at the heart of the city, a feminine figure approached in the distance, silhouetted by the blood moon behind her. Her presence brought with it a sense of ominous tension, accompanied by the distant howls of stray dogs and the rustling of trash blown by the wind.

"Scutum Fidei!" I cried, summoning my shield of faith just as a repetitive demonic force crashed over me, each concussive wave striking like the beat of a drum. The relentless onslaught threatened to hurl me backward, but my shield of light held firm, the only thing keeping me grounded amid the eerie silence of the deserted street.

The mysterious woman, her aura the source of the concussive waves of demonic force, paused and tilted her head, her movements curious. The air was thick with the scent of ozone, mingled with the faint odor of sulfur emanating from her demonic presence.

"You have power…" Her voice seemed to caress my ear even from this distance, so soft that it sent a shiver through my body, momentarily flickering my shield of golden light. Her voice seemed familiar to me somehow, echoing in the stillness of the night like a haunting melody.

Teeth clenched, I dug my heels into the pavement, bracing against the waves of demonic blasts that seemed to reverberate through the very ground beneath me. "Show me more," she cooed, her eyes glinting with a lustful gleam.

The next set of blasts came wreathed in hellfire, casting eerie shadows that danced along the empty storefronts lining the street. My heart raced, eyes widening in panic, as the distant wails of sirens mingled with the chaotic symphony of the supernatural.

"I can feel the strength of your faith. But for how long can it protect you?" The mysterious woman said, her voice cutting through the cacophony like a knife through the darkness. Without Simon, I had only one option. I bowed my head, closed my eyes, and prayed for deliverance.

"In the name of the Father, the Son, and the Holy Spirit, deliver me, O Lord, from this evil…" The sounds of her onslaught grew distant, fading into a faint whump, whump, whump.

As I prayed, a stinging wind lashed my face, carrying with it the distant scent of rain mingled with the metallic tang of blood.

The mysterious woman continued to taunt me, "Even you will be unable to stop what is coming. The mother of demons will be among us soon, and all will be as it should be."

"Keep me, O Lord, from the hands of the wicked," I continued, the words of my prayer a desperate plea against the encroaching darkness. "I pray for deliverance from this evil in Jesus' name, Amen."

My shield suddenly shattered, the wind ceasing abruptly. Leaves kicked up around me that weren't there before and fluttered back down to the grass on which I now stood. Opening my eyes, I saw that the mysterious woman was nowhere to be found. I was safe. For now.

My heart still raced from the confrontation with Rebecca, now the Antichrist, the woman shrouded in darkness. Disoriented and unsure of what to do or where to go, I stumbled through the quiet, dimly lit streets as Rebecca's voice echoed within my mind. "Coward," it said over and over again.

The eerie glow of the blood moon cast long red shadows, distorting my perception of my surroundings. I needed to find Simon to warn him and plan our next move.

After several minutes of disoriented wandering, I spotted a familiar figure standing in a small, secluded park below a streetlight, poring over an old paper. A raven perched on his shoulder, its sharp eyes scanning the area.

"Simon!" I called out, my voice hoarse from the struggle. Simon looked up, his eyes widening in surprise. He quickly rolled up the map and rushed toward me. "Jaydon! Thank God, you're safe. What happened? I felt a surge of demonic energy and feared the worst."

I took a deep breath, trying to steady myself. "Rebecca, it's Rebecca. She's the Antichrist, the chosen leader of the Cult of Lilith. She attacked me, but I managed to escape using a prayer of deliverance. We need to find her, Simon. We need to stop her. She plans to summon the mother of demons from across the veil!"

Terror passed over Simon's face before hardening into an intense look of determination. "Do you know where she might have gone?" he asked.

I closed my eyes and listened intently to the urgent whispering coming from the Ring of Solomon.

"She and her cultists are gathering in an abandoned building. Here, in the city," I said.

Simon quickly unrolled the enchanted map again, this time laying it flat on the ground. He knelt in front of it. He muttered an incantation, and the map began to shimmer, revealing intricate pathways and locations across the city. He traced his finger over the map, searching for a place that resonated with the darkest energy we had encountered yet.

"There," Simon said, pointing to a building on the outskirts of the city. "It's an old factory, long abandoned, and perfect for a cult gathering. The energy emanating from it matches what you described."

I nodded, a sense of urgency propelling me forward. "Let's go. We're already out of time."

We hurried through the Detroit streets, passing the city's occasional night stalker. As we approached the outskirts, the air grew colder, and an oppressive atmosphere began to settle over us. We arrived at the decrepit factory. Its structure looms ominously against the night sky. Faint, flickering lights could be seen through the broken windows, and the sound of chanting echoed from within.

As we navigated through the rubble and debris leading up to the entrance of the abandoned factory, I could feel the oppressive energy from within intensifying—a palpable sense of dread filling the air.

We reached the entrance and paused, steeling ourselves for what lay within. "Ready?" Simon asked.

I nodded, gripping my Star of David talisman where it rested on the outside of the chest of my dark gray peacoat. "Ready. Let's put an end to this."

My heart skipped a beat as we pushed open the creaking door of the factory, stepping into the darkness of the formerly abandoned building.

CHAPTER 15

The Antichrist's Ritual

The factory's interior sprawled vastly, its walls adorned with strange, glowing symbols akin to those marking every site of possessed candidates we'd encountered. Cultists in assorted colored robes, all female, encircled Rebecca. I recognized the two witches from the warehouse district among them.

The woman shrouded in darkness stood at the heart of a makeshift altar, surrounded by twisted candles lit with black flames that somehow still illuminated the room, dark stones adorned with sigils, and other ritualistic artifacts laid out in a circle surrounding the alter. Her eyes were ablaze with an unholy fervor that fixated on us, a wicked smile stretching across her face.

As I met her gaze, a shiver ran down my spine. Her eyes pierced through the shadows shrouding her, crackling with an ominous and powerful energy.

"Ah, the faithful and the wicked have arrived. Welcome. You're just in time for the ritual," she intoned as we entered the cavernous room.

Her voice cut through the air, chilling and commanding, addressing the entire assembly: "My mother, Lilith, is soon to pass through the veil and into this world. She will end all war, famine, and pestilence. We'll have no need for mortal leadership or politics under her reign. We shall finally know true world peace, the true meaning of 'love thy neighbor.'"

With Simon by my side, I stepped forward. I steadied my voice despite the palpable tension. "We won't let that happen. Your lies and blasphemy will not stand."

Before I could react, the woman shrouded in darkness unleashed a surge of demonic energy at me, but Simon anticipated it. With a flicker of arcane magic, he redirected the torrent of demonic energy toward himself.

In a fleeting moment, I caught Simon looking directly into my eyes as he redirected the torrent. His eyes were soft with acceptance, sure of his immediate decision. It was as if he were saying goodbye. He gave me his most playfully mischievous grin, even now.

Faster than I could blink, the blast broke through the protective barrier I had placed upon him back at the concrete bridge. As the blast of demonic energy consumed him, it left only a haunting silhouette flickering on the wall behind me.

I stared in shock at the spot where Simon had been standing only moments ago. Grief clenched my heart as I stared at the empty space where my friend once stood. The sudden loss weighed heavily on me.

"You see?" Her voice dripped with cruel satisfaction. "Your resistance is futile. Darkness will always triumph."

Refusing to yield, I summoned the ancient power of the Ring of Solomon, its energy pulsating along my hand and arm. With determination, I unleashed a blinding torrent of light, a beacon of defiance amid the encroaching darkness. The brilliance of light was absorbed by the shroud of darkness enveloping her.

"You cannot defeat me!" Rebecca's form contorted with rage, her dark powers swirling like a tempestuous storm.

"I may not prevent Lilith's rise," I admitted. "But I will stop you," I declared.

As I faced Rebecca, the embodiment of darkness, my heart pounded with fear and determination. Simon's sacrifice weighed heavily, but I couldn't falter now. With trembling hands, I reached for the power and wisdom of the Ring of Solomon once more, its power surging through me like a raging river.

A whisper echoed within my mind; it was a prayer, ancient and powerful. As if spoken by God himself.

With unwavering faith, I closed my eyes and spoke the prayer aloud. The words flowed, resonating with the ring's divine energies.

The prayer unleashed a brilliant holy light, burning away the darkness cloaking Rebecca. I watched in awe as the darkness receded, revealing her true essence beneath. Rebecca let out a primal scream as the light engulfed her, her form writhing in agony as the evil within her was cast out.

With a final burst of energy, she collapsed to the floor, her once formidable presence reduced to nothing more than a mere mortal for the last time.

The shadowy figure of the Antichrist loomed over her, its malevolent presence casting an ominous pall over the room.

Exhausted, I watched the shadowy figure lower itself to the floor beside Rebecca. It peered down at her unconscious form, then at me as the glow of the ring of Solomon dimmed and went out.

The room was silent as the members of the Cult of Lilith watched intently from the walls, keeping out of their cult leader's way.

The Antichrist's shadow essence slowly stalked over to me. As it did so, the glowing symbols covering every inch of the walls and floor of the factory began to move toward the Antichrist shadow essence as it crossed the room, absorbing all of the symbols into itself. Its humanoid body is now completely covered in the glowing symbols; it just stood in front of me, as if considering me for something. Then it reached forward and plunged its hand into the Star of David talisman on my chest. I began to scream as the Star of David talisman around my neck began to glow, vibrating violently. It's ancient protective energies fighting against the Antichrist's shadow essence, attempting to prevent it from doing whatever it was trying to do.

The power of the Star of David and the Ring of Solomon combined created a shockwave that threw the Antichrist's shadow essence across the room. It caught itself in mid-air; having absorbed enough energy from my talisman, it burst into an inky, pitch-black mist.

As it spread all throughout the room, enveloping even the cultists who stood watching, I knew this fight wasn't over yet as the inky darkness surrounded me.

But amid that darkness, amid the chaos and uncertainty, a glimmer of hope remained. My ancient artifacts had proven their power, and though the battle was far from won, I knew that with courage and perseverance, we could still emerge victorious against the forces of darkness that sought to take over my city and, from there, the world itself.

CHAPTER 16

A Light within the Darkness

As the darkness crawled toward me, a strange sense of clarity washed over me. In the midst of the encroaching shadows, I realized with a start that this was the vision Simon had warned me about back at the Church of Solomon—the moment when I would willingly allow the darkness to consume me.

For a brief moment, I hesitated, feeling the weight of uncertainty and fear pressing down on me. But then, amid the coming darkness, a flicker of understanding ignited within me. This was not a moment of surrender but rather a test of faith—a chance to confront the darkness head-on.

With newfound resolve, I closed my eyes and lowered my head. I began to pray silently as I allowed the darkness to swallow me like a tidal wave as everything suddenly fell silent.

The only light came from the symbols glowing faintly. Memories of those I had failed flashed through my mind, each one a painful reminder of the battles I had fought and lost.

I thought of Rebecca, whom I was unable to keep safe from the darkness that sought to claim her.

I thought of Daniel, whose promise to keep his sister safe ended in failure.

I thought of the woman we attempted to save from demonic possession back at the abandoned concrete bridge, her soul taken by the demon that had consumed her.

Finally, I thought of Simon, whose heroic sacrifice left nothing behind except a shadow flickering upon the wall of the factory.

Suddenly, the glowing symbols surrounding me within the endless darkness began to blink out and disappear, leaving me within an absolute void where I couldn't tell if my eyes were closed or open.

Within the now absolute darkness, I found a moment to reflect on my own shortcomings and on the weight of responsibility that rested upon my shoulders. But as the cold chill of the darkness seeped into every fiber of my being, I felt a profound sense of peace wash over me—a peace born not of surrender but of acceptance. Of forgiveness.

I opened my eyes as my Star of David talisman began to glow. Faintly at first, it gradually grew brighter and brighter until it could be seen through the pitch of that endless darkness. Through the light that shone from my talisman, within the darkness, I could see the face of an impeccably beautiful and well-endowed woman with platinum blonde hair, fair skin, and bright blue eyes. This was the face of Lilith herself, the mother of demons.

She smiled a genuine, caring smile. One of those smiles that couldn't possibly hide a single ounce of malice. But I knew it was deceitful.

I held my hand up in front of my face, the ring of Solomon facing Lilith within the darkness, glowing and vibrating with its divine power. I didn't say any of the words it whispered to me. Not this time. No, this time, I did it all myself.

"In the authority of the wise King Solomon, I command you, Lilith, to obey me. Hear my prayer!" I declared, my words ringing out with a clarity that belied the weight of the moment. "I bind the demon grouping known as Lilit, Lilith, Lamie, and all spirits known as Lilu, lilitu, Irdu lili, and Ardat lilit."

With each syllable, I could feel the power of ancient prayers coursing through me, fueling the chains of holy light that shot forth through the inky darkness, wrapping around Lilith's arms and binding her essence.

"I bind the spirits of lust and temptation, of pride and rebellion. The spirits of child sacrifice and the accusation that desire to rule over all nations," I continued, my voice steady despite the enormity of the task.

Another chain of holy light shot through the darkness and shackled Lilith. The combined power of my talisman's protection, of the ring of Solomon's divine energy, and of the Holy Spirit within me fueled my determination.

"Lilith, mother of demons, she-demon fiend who refused to comply nor obey Adam," I thundered, my voice echoing through the darkness. "Obey me now. I banish you in the name of our *Lord Jesus Christ!*"

My words reverberated with power, carrying the weight of centuries of faith and conviction. As the final syllable fell from my lips, Lilith was thrown back into the darkness as that same darkness surrounding me trembled, giving way to a blinding burst of light and warmth that consumed Lilith after I spoke the final word of my prayer: "Amen."

The darkness suddenly shattered like glass, leaving behind only echoes of Lilith's presence.

I found myself back in the factory building. The light of the rising sun shone through the windows of the factory. The cultists surrounding the room were now all unconscious. I fell to my knees, exhausted, focusing on my breathing. It was done. The Antichrist and leader of the Cult of Lilith were defeated, and Lilith herself was successfully prevented from fully emerging into our world. For if I— no, we—were to have failed, there was no telling what kinds of chaos and calamity Lilith and the Antichrist could have wrought.

With the darkness finally overcome and the biblical prophecy foretelling the coming of both the Antichrist and Lilith having come to fruition, an evil destiny thwarted, I took Rebecca home for the final time and returned to my hallowed sanctuary on the outskirts of the city of Detroit.

CHAPTER 17

A Departed Friend's Echo

The next day, I returned to the abandoned factory building to pay my respects to Simon, who had sacrificed his own life in order to save mine from the Antichrist. His shadow still lingered, a silent witness to our conflict from the previous day.

As I stood before the shadow of my late friend, I bowed my head and prayed for God to keep him close. Despite Simon being a wizard, a being associated with secrets, lies, and the pursuit of power, I prayed for his passage through the gates of heaven and into paradise among the angels. I had learned that he was not merely a seeker of power but a man devoted to the relentless pursuit of knowledge to protect those without power from the darkness.

I opened my eyes as a disembodied wind blew throughout the room. Simon's shadow suddenly detached itself from the wall, swirling into an orb of shadow before taking the form of a raven I recognized as Corvin, Simon's familiar. Its beady eyes, as piercing and intelligent as ever, locked onto mine just as Simon's voice shattered the silence.

"Well done, my friend. Well done," he said, clapping slowly as I turned to face him.

"Simon?" I said, shocked. "You're really here?"

"In the flesh," he said, flashing me his most playfully mischievous grin as Corvin flew over and perched itself upon his shoulder.

"But... but you were vaporized by the Antichrist... how did..." I started.

"You know," Simon began, "a wise pastor once said, 'Some things are better left unknown.'"

I embraced my friend in a hug and slapped him hard on the back. He wasn't some ghost, apparition, or vision. He really was here. I didn't bother to ask how.

FINAL SCENE

Simon's Song

Simon found himself wandering the streets of Detroit, his mind heavy with the weight of his recent sacrifice. The decision to rely on a dangerous and rare form of familiar magic, despite the consequences, had left him imbued with demonic energy. He knew full well the dangers that awaited him, his inner demons literally threatening to consume him entirely.

As he walked, he came upon the Detroit Cathedral, its ancient stones weathered by time and consecrated by faith.

Inside, the hallowed halls echoed with the haunting melody of Simon's voice.

Alone, standing before the pulpit where a sculpture of Jesus Christ hung upon a cross, Simon raised his clasped hands in supplication, his eyes closed in fervent prayer.

"Tell me what you want from me. Tell me what you wanna see. I'll show you everything—the voices calling me over and over again," Simon confessed, his heart heavy with the weight of his burden.

Yet as he continued to confess his sins, his voice grew stronger with each impassioned plea for forgiveness.

"Forgive me, my mother. Forgive me, my father. Forgive me, my brother. For I know not what I do."

His words reverberated through the grand sanctuary of the cathedral, carrying with them a potent mix of both emotion and raw magic. The stained glass windows bathed him in a kaleidoscopic glow.

"Forgive me, my mother!" he cried out, his voice echoing off of the ancient walls of the cathedral's sanctuary. "Forgive me, my father! Forgive me, my brother! For I know not what I've done!"

As his prayerful song reached its crescendo, the voices in his head continued their relentless assault, their whispers a cruel reminder of his own inner turmoil.

"You're not a hero," the voices hissed, the words like venom in his ears. "You're a devil, not a saint. Your words are lethal. You think you're Abel, yet you're Cain. You'll always be Cain."

But amid the chaos of his own mind, Simon found a glimmer of hope. With his voice raised in prayerful song, he offered up his sins to the heavens. Sins he hadn't even known he'd already committed.

ABOUT THE AUTHOR

Grant Hazen resides in Saginaw, Michigan, with his familiar, a tabby cat named Nazareth (Nazzy) Maple. Grant is a Christian with a love for his family, his Lord and Savior Jesus Christ, and a fascination for the mysterious and unexplainable. In other words, Grant is a geek. A geek who knew there had to be more to life than working retail. In all honesty, Grant at first wanted nothing to do with reading and writing. He was often quizzed on the chapters of books he had to read as homework for school assignments because he was prone to skipping pages. Eventually, Grant stumbled upon a series of six books that beckoned to him as if God himself were nudging him toward a future of becoming an author. God truly works in mysterious ways.